Memories

Of

Seventeen

By Alfred Brock

This book is composed of poems that I wrote when I was seventeen.

I was living in Elmhurst, New York at the time. Elmhurst is part of New York City and is located in Queens Borough on Long Island.

The poems were written at home, travelling around the city or at various places around the city.

These were written at the end of 1978 and the early part of 1979.

Straight Into Monday

I'm so smashed

I can't see

I'm wonderin'

Where I'll be

In five minutes

I don't know

And now I don't care

I need another slug

To keep me goin'

I'm gonna' fly straight into Monday

<u>**Love me**</u>

Take me back

Please

I need you

So much

I'm cryin'

I need ya'!

Lazy

The bees are buzzin'

My head is clear

The trees are swayin'

And this meadow smells so sweet

I could lie here forever

And think

About the sun

About the clouds

About the blue sky

About myself

Just drowsin'

I'll stay a while longer

Until the stars come out

They're so pretty

A while more

The sun's comin'

Just let me lie here

A while longer

A while longer

A while longer

Yes.

<u>**Four Seasons**</u>

Hey Four Seasons

Your music is light mellow

Your guitarist is easy

Your bassist is in

Your man on keyboards hangs out

But your drummer

He's the coolest

A clean cut non-conformist

He's our man

<u>**Chinook**</u>

Fly, chopper, fly

Fly so high

That I can't see you

Fly so high

That the enemy won't see you

Swoop down

Kill him

Fly away

Clutching your prey to your belly

Hold them fast

The dropping point is coming up

It's green and hilly

Our enemy's friends are down there

Hiding

Release the bodies

There

They fall

Spiraling

So slowly

So prettily

And the horror they bring

Is nothing

Compared to the fleeting moment of beauty

Now, chopper, now

Rise,

No,

They've hit you

Beautiful angel

Machine of war

You are in your final throes

You burn orange

A ball of light

The men tumble

The Chinook has passed

Harriet

Harriet, Harriet,

Where have you gone,

Are you out dancing,

Are you out singing,

Are you out drinking,

Are you out having fun,

Why don't you come home,

Harriet, Harriet.

Moon Lake Cathedral

Moon Lake Cathedral,

Where art thee now,

Did you burn to the ground,

Or did you,

Fall into the sea,

Did the sky swallow you up,

Where are you,

You took my lover,

Where are you.

Lost Love at Moon Lake Cathedral

Lover, I found you,

Lover, I lost you,

Moon Lake Cathedral,

Looked so beautiful,

At dawn,

The mists hung about her,

Like a wedding gown,

We saw it from the boat,

Before we landed,

When we landed,

We were so happy,

And then the cloud,

But I had to go,

I did,

Wandering is in my soul,

You wouldn't let me go,

You went down to the lake,

And left,

Why, why,

Did you go.

<u>**Daisy**</u>

Daisy, you are so simple,

You are so bright,

Yellow, and brown, and green,

A Tri-colored angel,

You are,

You are lovely,

And simple.

<u>Forgotten Wharf</u>

Downtrodden New Yorker,

You are so alone,

God abandoned you,

To the waves,

You hang out,

On the beach,

Out of the reach,

Of the sun,

In the winter,

The water's cold,

You don't go in,

Or it would take you,

Away,

To warmer places,

New homes,

New friends,

Good friends,

Eat heartily of the meal,

You fixed for yourself,

Be one,

With the elf,

That caused you,

To die,

You've forgotten,

The warmth of Miami,

The fun of L.A.,

The mellowness of New Orleans,

You only remember,

The freezing winds,

You match the climate,

With your mind,

And,

With your heart.

Electrical Light

The sharpness of the glass,

Is in tomorrow,

And it is in eternity,

Forever it will exist,

In, and on,

The pyramid,

Mathematical equations,

Are flying by,

And they close my mind,

To the slopes,

Of Mt.Nowl,

Forever.

<u>**Future Beings**</u>

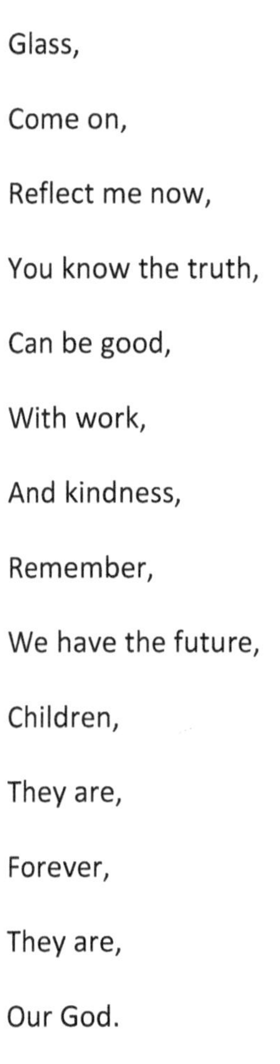

Glass,

Come on,

Reflect me now,

You know the truth,

Can be good,

With work,

And kindness,

Remember,

We have the future,

Children,

They are,

Forever,

They are,

Our God.

Big River of Life

Big River,

Ride me on,

To the sea,

I want to touch the sun,

If I float to the sky's edge,

I can climb the remainder,

Just take me there,

Over rocky rapids,

Waterfalls,

Still waters,

Run me deep,

Run me long,

There's always the sea,

To flow to,

It's so deep,

So cold,

So honest,

Despair runs off,

It won't run low,

It won't run deep,

It just can't,

The river doesn't take it,

It stands on love,

Even in winter,

When the sea freezes,

We see despair in retreat,

From the cold honesty of the river's heart,

The river is the life of the sea,

And the life of the river,

Is below the ground,

In the hollows of deep rock,

The water,

The life,

Rises,

Up,

Into the light,

It cleans the land,

And refreshes the sea,

The sky and sun,

Look on,

And they are pleased,

Because the river rolls on,

Riding me on,

Running me deep,

Running me low,

It's forever,

And free,

The river freezes,

But the life rolls on,

The river is solid,

And physical,

The love is flowing,

And mental,

That river,

Rolls on,

Through the plains,

Through the hills,

Through the valleys,

Through the mountains,

Through the clouds,

Through the sky,

Through the planets,

Though life,

And it rolls on,

And it is,

As a thing filled with goodness,

And it lives,

As it should be,

Because it is,

The river,

It runs low,

It runs deep,

It runs on.

Trees

Evening comes,

The light goes,

The trees breathe oxygen,

And they rest,

Man breathes oxygen,

Everyday,

We need friends,

We have friends,

In the trees.

<u>**The Children**</u>

Where is the night,

Has it run off,

Has it left us,

The day is so long,

It seem forever,

The darkness is here,

But the night,

It is still so far away,

The night,

It is not just the absence of light,

It is a rest from the day,

The day that is forever,

Night comes quickly,

The day has breached our defenses,

I can see no more,

The children are awake,

The lesson is not soon forgotten,

Everyone teaches it,

The night caresses it,

The day spurns it,

Peace is not the way of the day,

It is the meaning of night,

The night that won't come,

We beseech you,

Come to us,

Aid us,

In our hour of need,

Night, oh glorious night,

Remember the children,

They must rest,

They must learn,

Their's is the future,

Their's is the job of the future,

Lead them night,

Into your fond embrace,

And show them rest,

And intelligence,

Hide them from the day,

As long as you can,

But when will you arrive,

When will you arrive,

Night, come,

Blanket the world,

Comfort the leaders,

Rest the children,

Help us flee the day,

Be kind,

Be quick,

Dance to our sides,

Come in the morning,

Come in the evening,

Arrive and save us,

Rest the children.

Cowbell

Where ya' goin',

Mister Cowbell,

You follow the cow,

On home,

To food,

To life,

To love.

<u>**A Search for Being**</u>

Could the being,

Be here,

In space,

Where all is empty,

But man is full,

Yes, man is full,

He overflows,

Out onto the world,

His will spills,

Man changes,

Man changes things,

Man changes man,

And he returns,

To himself.

<u>**Look at Colors**</u>

Green is so silent,

Red is so silent,

White is so silent,

Black is so silent,

Blue is so silent,

Yellow,

       So silent,

The rainbow,

Is beautiful.

<u>Neil Young</u>

Play it forever, Neil Young,

Play it forever,

Live it forever,

The guitar,

The harmonica,

The piano,

The song,

Play it forever,

Grave yard man,

You wander about,

To the limits of the mind's soul's eye,

Into the zone,

Of life,

Music,

Play it forever,

It is you,

Neil,

You play the music,

The music is you,

Yes,

And you are the music,

Play it forever, Neil Young.

I left for a reason

Flag me down,

Lady,

Of the sky,

Remember me,

I came from the sky,

To return to the sea,

And to forget,

You,

Lady.

Long life

Whoa,

Ease up,

Don't slip down,

You're gonna' fall,

Down,

So down,

It's a fall,

Not forgotten,

Go on,

For years,

And live on,

For years.

The 60's

I was just in time,

To see the world end,

I lived through it,

But I learn about it,

I didn't look around,

And I want to learn about,

And remember,

My early life,

The end of the world.

<u>You Life</u>

Be sweet,

Be silent,

Be good,

Be steadfast,

Be right,

Be smart,

Be fast,

Be all,

Be God,

And pass on.

The Sea

I'll run around,

Just tonight,

Down to the sands,

Of the sea,

I'll run around,

Just tonight,

Down to the rocks,

Of the sea,

I'll run around,

Just tonight,

Down to the life,

Of the sea.

I'm going to the celebration

I'm all jammed,

I'll never move along,

To the quarter,

In New Orleans,

You know that parade,

And party,

It is so good,

Mardi Gras is quick,

Fat Tuesday est blanc

And it exists,

In Louisiana, U.S.A.,

In the people,

There.

Universe

Hey Universe,

You are so forever,

And unknown,

You are me,

My mind is in you,

My friends are in you,

You are in you,

You are good,

You are forever.

<u>**'78**</u>

Happy year,

You've been good,

You've been bad,

But I'm just glad,

That I've been,

With my people,

      People.

<u>**For Geri**</u>

Pretty eyes of the girl,

Pretty eyes of the boy,

Meet,

Pretty mouth of the girl,

Pretty mouth of the boy,

Meet,

Pretty hands of the girl,

Pretty hands of the boy,

Meet,

Pretty mind of the girl,

Pretty mind of the boy,

Touch.

Future

Oh, leave m e,

Desert me,

Oh, forget me,

      Ignore me,

For that and all else,

      Are gone,

      Me.

A fact

Don't forget,

I've been here,

Though I've moved on,

I've been here,

Though I may forget,

I've been here,

It won't change,

I've been here.

The World

Be happy,

And smile at the world,

The world is happy,

It smiles at you,

It gives you air to breathe,

It gives you food to eat,

It gives you drink to drink,

      It gives you people to love,

         While you're here.

Desert

Desert,

I'm comin' to ya',

'Cause the place I left,

Is much too cold,

And much to small,

The people,

Millions,

Are so very lonely,

They can't pick their way,

It's forced on them,

Their faces flow,

As it suits the time of day,

But the masks fall away,

When the sun drops,

When actions are hidden,

And men fear that they may be next,

    In line,

Desert, help me,

Desert, hide me,

I'll help you,

Protect you from the others,

From the unreal ones,

We'll run together.

<u>Green Vein</u>

Green vein flow,

Green vein kill,

Carry the poison,

Bringing confusion,

Save me,

      Gone,

            Poisoned,

            Green vein.

<u>Job</u>

Grow flower,

And live,

Give your seed,

And die,

The earth loves you,

And it cares for you,

But you must work,

And you do,

      You are beautiful,

         Full-time.

Baby

I really, really thought,

I wouldn't forget,

About that time,

About that place,

Down in the quarter,

Where the grits were so white,

And you eyes were so blue,

Your body was a joy,

      Pure simplicity,

You reached out to me,

I reached out to you,

We met, We touched,

But I moved on, I lost you,

I was a fool,

But the road,

It's voice commanded me,

I couldn't resist,

The road,

It pulled me away,

From you,

I'll never forget again,

Neer

I really, really believe that.

<u>Hey, V.</u>

Come with me,

To L.A.,

Where we can love,

Down by the waves,

In the tall, cool dunes,

We can become one,

There,

In that city,

We'll be no fools,

Never separate from one another,

Come with me,

I love you.

Darling

You'll never know,

Who I am,

Unless you try,

To see me,

Where I am,

I dwell in the night,

I dwell in the day,

I work on the river,

I work on the bank,

Look for me,

Already,

I see you.

<u>**I have to go**</u>

Amber,

You are so beautiful,

You talk long,

Your words are like song,

But my feet,

You cannot bind,

I must roll on,

To the end of this asphalt fate,

    Of mine,

I must find the answer,

    In the end,

        Somewhere.

<u>**Europe**</u>

Europe, you are far away,

From me,

I'll be there,

Not soon,

With my love,

But you are my hope,

I will see you,

And feel you,

Europe,

You still are,

Europe.

<u>**Across from her house**</u>

That café,

That sangria,

Tastes so good,

    So sweet,

    So fine,

    The sun,

Cascading,

    Blinds me,

    Burns me,

      Protects me,

And makes me feel good.

Ribbon

Ribbon, flow,

Ribbon, fall,

Ribbon, Roll,

Ribbon, Cascade,

Ribbon, be,

Ribbon, Ribbon,

Ribbon,

Ribbons in her hair,

Ribbons.

<u>**Wind**</u>

Blow wind blow,

Cool my soul,

I'm on fire,

My baby left me,

And I don't know what

       to do,

I'm all keyed up,

       Cool me off.

Road-man

Where ya' gonna' be today,

If ya' go,

I'll fade away,

I'll fall to my knees,

And fail,

And fail to be me,

You know how I feel,

    It's so real,

    Why you gonna' run,

    Stay, and have some fun,

    The road's not strong,

    No, you're wrong,

    It's not,

    Stay with me,

    Don't go,

    Be slow,

    Stay, don't go away,

        Good-bye.

<u>Not</u>

Is that the dance I do,

I don't want to learn it,

Is that the book I read,

I don't want to read it,

Is that the thing I do,

I don't want to do it,

Is that the person I have to be,

I don't want to be it,

     I'm leaving,

     Here,

     Forever.

<u>**Give me a beer**</u>

Call me No man,

Call me dude from L.A.,

The head from Orleans,

Just don't tie me down,

Don't tie me down.

<u>**3 weeks time**</u>

Are you leavin' me again,

      Will if you are,

Here's where I be,

In 3 weeks time,

'Cause I know,

You'll be back,

      Yes, you'll be back,

'Cause you know,

You can't really leave me,

      I know the backroads,

I'm your key to the beauty of America,

      Yes, you'll be back,

      You'll be back,

      Within 3 weeks time,

      I'll be seein' your pixie face,

      In your frilly lace,

      You love what I know,

         You love me,

            Here's my address woman,

Here's where I'll be,

In 3 weeks time,

'Cause I know,

You'll be back,

By my side,

A cryin,

For me to take you back,

And we'll go on,

Right down the road,

You and me,

'Cause I love ya',

And you love me,

And here's where I'll be,

In 3 weeks time,

'Cause I know,

You'll be back,

In my loving arms,

In 3 weeks time.

<u>**Rest, honey**</u>

You ain't got to work no more, woman,

    You got me now,

And I'll pay your way baby,

Can't you see,

You got me now,

    And your future is easy and bright,

'Cause you got me now,

So, sit right back,

And love me good,

'Cause you ain't got to work no more,

    You got me now,

        You worked all your life,

        Scratchin' the soil,

        Well I'm no fat cat,

    But I get by,

And you ain't gonna' work no more,

    You got me now,

    And I love you.

<u>**New day**</u>

New day,

I've finally arrived,

I've been travelling so long,

To find you,

New day,

I've walked through the sad days,

I've staggered through the grey days,

I've stumbled through bad days,

    To reach you,

        Here,

            New day.

<u>**In praise of a time for Blues**</u>

Well Bach,

And Beethoven,

      They're fine for worship,

But when I'm drinking beer,

And when my baby's left me again,

Give some lonesome, southern blues,

'Cause they are,

What I am right now,

Lonesome and Blue.

<u>Tijuana dirt road</u>

Tijuana,

You are so hot,

I think I'll have a little Sangria,

The music is low and sweet,

And my head is fuzzy,

It's cooling off,

I think I'll have a little beer,

The bus it outside,

Windows down,

People out,

Cooling off during their stop,

In Tijuana,

I think I'll have a little Sangria,

Mexican guitars playing on the porches,

They're making me cry,

I think I'll have a little beer,

I'll take a walk down the road,

To talk with the village men,

Let the sun beat down,

We're in the shade,

On a porch,

Havin' fun,

I think I'll have a little Sangria.

<u>No blindness</u>

Well drinkin' is fine,

But when you can't see,

Well,

I only drink till I'm fuzzy,

Then I mellow out,

I want memories,

And one way or another,

I'm gonna' get 'em.

Writing and walking

Well, politics not for me,

Much too boring,

And I don't want to be an engineer,

Nor a doctor,

Not an athlete,

Not a pilot,

I don't want to drive a truck,

    For a living,

And I don't want to write for a living,

I will live for writing,

    And nothing more,

    And nothing less.

<u>**Lost on the street**</u>

Brown bag, Brown bag,

     Where do you go,

Brown bag, Brown bag,

     Where do you walk,

Brown bag, Brown bag,

     Where do you fly,

Brown bag, Brown bag,

     Lost on the street.

<u>Lie</u>

I'm getting along,

Without you,

I got Jesus in my pocket,

And the bus is pulling in,

I'm getting along,

Loneliness bites at my heels,

I have no companion to chase it away,

I'm getting along,

Talking to myself,

Leads nowhere,

I'm getting along,

Without you,

I'm a terrible liar.

<u>**A dream**</u>

My medal in my pocket,

Keeps me safe,

It feels good,

When God is physical,

When you can touch him,

In holy things,

My medal in my pocket.

Train

Hey, Train,

Take me away,

Down your lonely tracks,

To the sea,

I want to swim in the Pacific,

I'm bored,

So ride me off,

To the sun,

On your magic ribbons in the sun,

Train, Train,

Be magic,

And,

Let me off.

<u>**Jason**</u>

I'm everyone's son,

'Cause I'm everyone's brother,

    So hold on,

The moon's not far away,

Just step inside,

Across the street,

And we'll be one.

John-boy

You stand tall and bright,

     You're a believer,

You can write,

You dream of Rockfish,

You moved to New York,

But the mountain is in you,

And you'll always return,

And remember your younger days,

The Winters,

The Falls,

The Springs,

The Summers,

The beginnings,

Oh, the memories come flooding back,

First loves,

First jobs,

And then you leave,

Only to return,

Again,

And again,

And again.

Triangle

Turn around,

Stand on your head,

You're the same,

You never change,

But you're always moving,

Incredible,

Triangle.

3 minutes left

One hundred,

And eight seconds left,

Don't skip,

Don't jump,

This has quite a ways to go,

N.C.,

It may be,

Grit your teeth,

Hold your breath,

The stones,

Three minutes

South

Forget me here,

I'm pulling out,

This town's not me,

It's much too cold,

I'm losing my hold,

I'm heading South,

To Jamaica,

Then Jacksonville,

North,

Warm North,

It's too cold this far north,

The good stuff is stouth,

On the bayou,

On the beach,

In the jungle,

<u>**Boots**</u>

I'm gonna' put on my boots,

And walk right out,

    Right out of this town,

    I'm down,

    So walk me out,

    Boots,

    Walk me out.

<u>**Here**</u>

Curl up,

And sleep forever,

Stand up,

And walk forever,

Spread my wings,

And fly forever,

Take off,

Into the eternity of eternities,

I'll just lie down,

And become the beginning,

I'll just be,

And become the end,

And leave,

Here.

Girl

Pardon my arm,

Woman,

Have a beer,

On me,

Come to room,

That's nice,

So nice,

Goodbye,

I'm leavin' now,

For Mexico,

Lady-woman.

Earth

Plow the field,

Smell the earth,

Feel the dirt,

It is alive,

It reaches up,

And gives food,

It will never be tamed,

It's always the saem,

    The Earth.

<u>Change</u>

Modernization,

Liberation,

Mechanization,

Nation,

Colonization,

I'm getting tired of –ation,

Change.

Chicago

Chicago,

You're cold,

    And icy,

I'm warm,

But you will chill me,

Others will enjoy you,

Not I,

I think.

It becomes water

Ice cream,

You be so cold,

Like the North,

Where the freezin' wind blows,

And a' whistles,

'Cross the tundra,

Out to the Ice,

Of the Pole,

Of the cap,

It all comes together,

And freezes,

    Together,

    The ice comes south,

    And becomes water,

    Loose, deep water,

        Water.

The Texan's Love

Well, if you love the Texan,

You better tell him,

Or he'll leave you,

      By morning,

He'll be back East,

Havin' a feast,

But if you want him to,

He'll stay on,

But his pocket is filled with cash,

His belly is filled with hash,

Catch him,

Catch him quick,

      And tell him.

Misapplied Blues

I look out the window,

On the second floor,

At the light a' flashin',

Hotel,

The lights are out,

My shirt is off,

I've a cigarette in my right hand,

A gun in my left,

There's a shot of whiskey,

On the table,

Next to the bottle,

That's next to the Bible,

The management left,

Blues are playin',

    On my pocket radio,

Misapplied Blues.

Hot summer Blues

Well the daisies in the window,

Are all stale and brown,

The whiskey's gone,

I need some bullets,

I'm leavin' tonight,

      To hit the road,

      This room's too small,

      And the window's broke,

      I grab my jacket and holster,

It's leather ya' know,

      Quite a smooth draw,

      And head for the door,

The quarter's too hot in summer,

In the winter,

The river don't smell,

And everyone wants to party,

But the summer's too slow,

Think I'll head for Denver,

It's cool there,

And I have to cool off,

For just a while,

Save that room, Clerk, 'cause I'll be back,

To the quarter and to life.

New York

When I die,

Take me back,

To New York,

'Cause when I'm lying in the grave,

I want somethin' solid around me,

And New York is solid,

Oh, New York is eternal,

'Cause she's ripe,

And the imagination runs wild,

And your soul is free,

    In New York,

    The Blues are in New Orleans,

    The Rock is in L.A.,

    The country is south,

    In New York,

    They're all together,

    And they're solid,

    Solid New York.

<u>Blues Basement Bar</u>

I can hardly breathe in here,

But the whiskey's good,

And the music's sad,

    So it's o.k.,

    Hey man,

    Play, "Shotgun Blues",

    'Cause it seems like rain to me,

    And can't you see,

    I got 'em,

    They're in my soul,

And I can't shake 'em,

So go ahead,

Play it,

Oh, yeah,

I can dig it,

Hey, Charlie,

I'll take a whole bottle,

And some shells too,

Yeah, Charlie, yeah,

I'll be seein' ya'.

New Orleans Blues

I'm sitting in L.A.,

Can't think of a thing to say,

    I've got these New Orleans Blues again,

    They're eatin' my brain,

    The Coast is getting' slow,

    I can't find no good action and New Orleans is lookin'

good,

    Again,

    Think I'll hop on the first freight east,

    I'm blowin' this town,

    New Orleans is a'waitin' for me,

    And I'll soon be there,

      Again,

    Ain't nothin' gonna' stop me,

    I ain't gonna' sleep till I arrive,

    Be damned,

    Yeah, be damned,

It I don't make it by Tuesday,

    I done it before,

And I'll do it,

Again,

Just to shake,

Those New Orleans blues,

That are heavy on my mind.

<u>I lost her there</u>

Rotting in the basement,

Is the picture,

Of her,

Holding some Tequila,

All bleary eyed,

Yes, all bleary eyed,

That trip to Mexico,

Just burned her out,

It laid her down,

Right down in the dust,

In the dust,

I lost her there.

<u>**Now that's Possible**</u>

Could it be,

She's gone,

Could it be,

She left me,

Could it be,

Someone took her place,

Could it be,

I'm happier now,

    Yes sir,

        It could be.

<u>**When the crocus blooms**</u>

When the crocus blooms,

A baby is born,

When the wind blows,

A man moves,

When the sun rises,

When the crocus blooms.

<u>**Cold**</u>

The way you did it,

Was like,

You took a gun,

And shot my head,

Everyone knows,

    You hurt me,

        You killed me,

            You untethered me,

            And I floated away,

            Away,

            Away.

She settled down

Don't bother me now,

Don't call me back,

The moon is risin',

And the sun is gone,

I don't want you anymore,

You don't want to run anymore,

The world was yours,

But you gave it back,

But I'm keepin' mine,

And I'll be goin'.

A taunt

Yes, the wine tastes sweeter,

Yes, the girls are prettier,

Yes, the work is light,

Yes, the sun is high,

Yes, the food is delicious,

    Yes, I am happy,

    How are you.

The Book

The words are empty,

And often misplaced,

But the feelings are full,

And in the right order,

Should I say more,

I think not.

How much does a dream cost

May I have a dime,

    To buy a gum,

    To buy a candy,

    To buy a treat,

    To buy a dream,

    Maybe two,

    They're only a nickel.

The world changes

Just because I don't agree,

You say I don't understand,

Maybe you don't understand,

That once you were right,

And now you are wrong,

The words cannot change,

But the world does.

I've got you

You've got to be crazy,

If you think,

You're gonna' beat me,

You've got to be crazy,

If you think,

You're gonna' hurt me,

And if I should lose ground,

I'll leave,

That's all.

<u>**Die**</u>

30 million,

40 million,

50 million,

Die,

You will anyway,

    Go ahead,

        Crawl away,

      Listen to the eternal voice,

        And die.

<u>Watered</u>

Hey, pot of flowers,

You run dry,

      I will water you,

Hey, bird,

You cry,

I will free you,

      Hey,

      You sigh,

      Watered.

<u>**I will**</u>

Think of it,

You will go,

Think of it,

     Before me,

     Think of it,

          I will outlast you,

          I will.

<u>Friends</u>

Forever friends,

Forever brothers,

Forever to gather,

For near,

Forever loving,

Forever caring,

      Forever remembering.

I'm so mean

When I die,

Well maybe heaven won't take me,

But, If they don't,

I'm sure I won't be able,

To retrace my steps,

That's how bad I am,

I do believe,

I'll get my own corner.

Quarter Blues

I'm so blue,

The whiskey don't burn,

I'm so blue,

The pot ain't sweet,

I'm so blue,

The cigarettes taste good,

I'm so blue,

I think I'll run to the quarter,

And let my sorrows,

Run off there,

> The blues don't stay long,

> In the quarter,

> They just fall away,

> But, when they're gone,

> You don't hang around,

>> Or they'll be back with you,

> In the quarter,

> And then,

> Even if you're so blue,

The whiskey don't burn,

It will,

Even if you're so blue,

The pot ain't sweet,

It is,

Even if you're so blue,

The cigarette taste good,

They won't,

And if that happens,

Then you go the Quarter Blues,

And they don't leave ya',

No, they don't leave,

But your sould will.

Diligence

If you been cheated so much,

You can't stand,

      Stand up,

If you been beaten so bad,

You can't speak,

      Shout,

'Cause you gotta' keep goin',

All the way.